For Joseph and Katy
**D.M**

For my parents, who fed me while I painted this
**K.H**

With special thanks to
Rachael Hemsley and Lisa MacKenzie
for their help and support

BRUSH ANIMAL
BOOKS

First published 2019 by Brush Animal Books

Glasgow, Scotland

www.brushanimal.com

ISBN: 978-1-9161910-0-6

Text copyright © David McGinty 2019

Illustrations copyright © Kirsty Hunter 2019

Moral rights asserted

All rights reserved. No part of this publication may be reproduced, stored in or introduced into a retrieval system, or transmitted in any form, or by any means (electronic, mechanical, photocopying, recording or otherwise) without the prior written permission of the publisher.

1 3 5 7 9 8 6 4 2

Printed in Glasgow, Scotland by Bell & Bain Limited

# I DON'T FEEL CHRISTMASSY YET

David McGinty

Illustrated by Kirsty Hunter

In place of the skeletons, witches, and cats
Was a man with a white beard, red suit, and hat.

Grace and her dad were out walking the streets
Enjoying the last of their Halloween sweets.

Now Christmas was coming, it wouldn't be long
But Grace wasn't excited...
　　　　　　　　　　something was wrong.

Surrounded by Santa, his elves, and reindeer

"No, surely," Grace thought, "he's too early this year."

She still felt the same...
and her toes were just wet!

"That's strange," she said.
"I don't feel Christmassy yet!"

A few weeks later December arrived
And Grace got a calendar with chocolates inside.
It came from her sister who lived far away
And it had little doors she could open each day.

At school, all the children wrote letters and lists
To send off to Santa requesting their gifts.

They wrote them politely,
just like they'd been taught

"But I feel like there's still something missing," Grace thought.

"I've asked for the presents I'm hoping to get
So how come I just don't feel Christmassy yet?"

"Shall we put up the tree?" Grace's mum asked one night
But when they were finished it wasn't quite right.

They'd hung all the baubles, the tinsel looked great,
But Mum said the star would "just have to wait".

"But why are we waiting?" Grace said to her mum
"We need to get ready for Santa to come!"

She loved this old family Christmas tradition

And while Mum queued up to pay the admission

Grace thought as she hummed to the bright festive tunes.

"I think this is it!
I'll feel Christmassy soon!"

But all through the film Mum and Dad laughed and cried

And heard not a peep from the girl by their side.

The ending was happy but Grace felt upset.
"I wonder why I don't feel Christmassy yet?"

While waiting one day to meet Santa in town
A few of his helpers had noticed her frown.

"Why won't you just smile, little girl?" asked an elf
As he pulled down a doll from the top grotto shelf.

"Look around, we're all happy! You shouldn't feel sad
Just take this toy and go home with your dad."

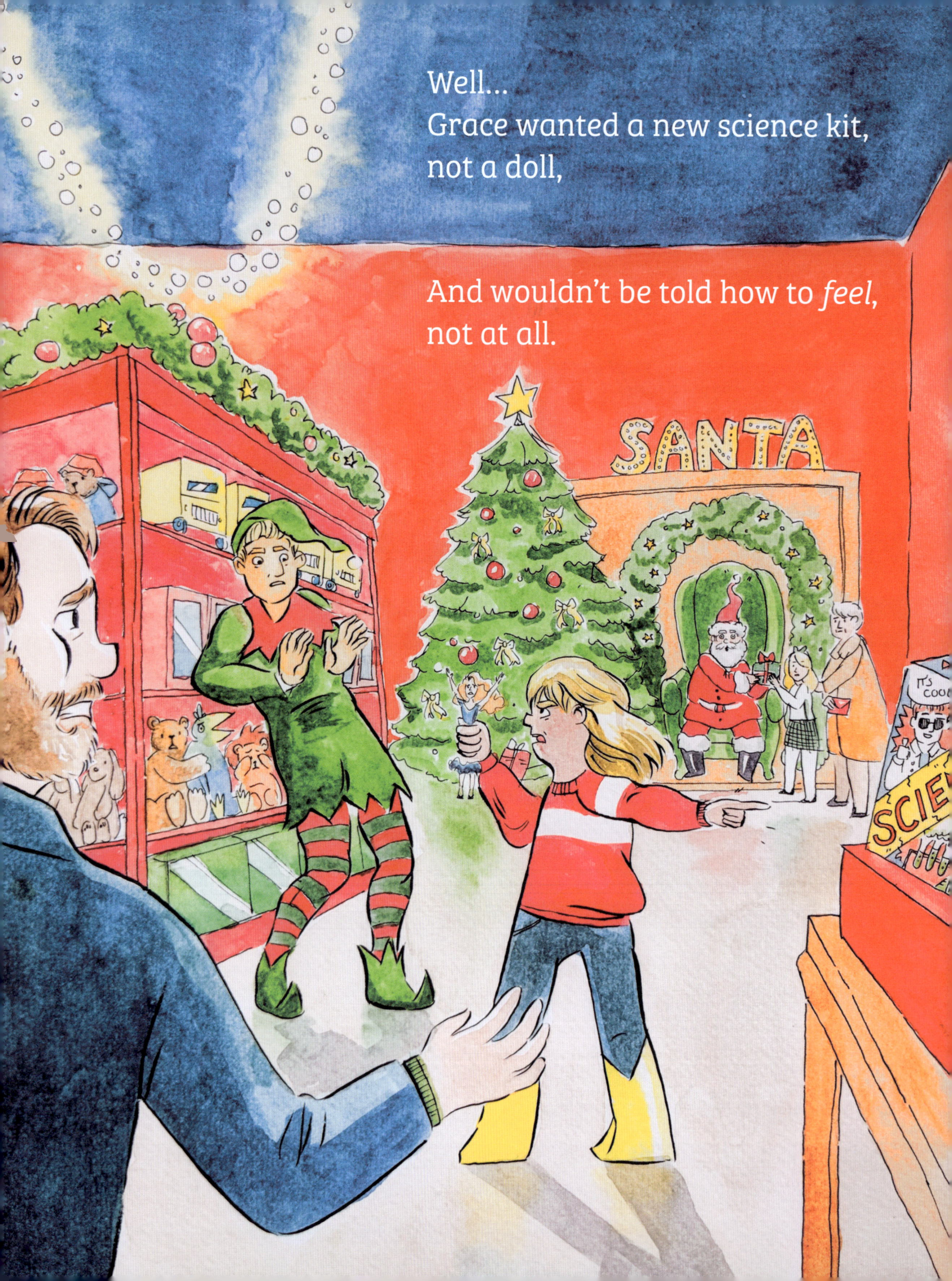

She'd always been told by her dad, "Be yourself."
So she thought she would tell off this terrible elf.

"I think you're the worst elf that I've ever met!
I can't help that **I don't feel Christmassy yet!**"

On that cold Christmas Eve, Grace sat on the stairs
And thought, as the following day was prepared

"Everyone feels Christmassy, everyone but me.
And there still isn't even a star on our tree!"

"What now? If I never love Christmas again,
Will that make me different from all of my friends?"

But just as her first tear splashed onto the floor...

a jangling of keys came from outside the door.

The front door burst open, to Grace's surprise!

She rubbed the wet tears
from her cheeks and her eyes.

With a cuddle so huge
that she nearly was crushed
Her sister was home,
Grace had missed her so much.

Now that all were together, that cold Christmas Eve...

They could finally put the gold star on the tree!

With her family around her, Grace said aloud
"I feel it at last! I feel Christmassy now!"